WRITTEN BY
SYLVESTER BARZEY

PARISH

AN EXTREME HORROR SHORT

SYLVESTER BARZEY

Copyright © 2024 by Sylvester Barzey

All rights reserved.

No part of this book may be reproduced in any form or by any electronic or mechanical means, including information storage and retrieval systems, without written permission from the author, except for the use of brief quotations in a book review.

CONTENTS

Introduction	vii
Parish	1
Neighbor	54
Don't Tell Grandma	60
Dead Soil Preview	64
Afterword	73
About the Author	75
Also by Sylvester Barzey	77

INTRODUCTION

Hey Survivor,

So in 2021, I was working on a project called "Parish" It was a short slasher story that I called Texas Chainsaw with Black women. Because of the subject matter and some of the characters I decided to send it out to a few close friends as sensitivity readers. The response I got back wasn't bad but it wasn't great, so I put Parish on the back burner.

Parish focuses on Police Brutality and Death at the hands of the police, which is something the Black community is dealing with in real time so I can totally understand why people won't want to tackle it in their fiction. It's heavy subject matter, so if it's not something you want to focus on or something you don't have the energy to deal with, I totally understand skipping this story.

Parish might be one of my darkest stories. I think it would fit more in extreme horror, but not too extreme. Nonetheless here are the Content Warnings for this story:

INTRODUCTION

- Racism
- Police Brutality
- Talks Of Sexual Assault
- Graphic Violence
- Elderly Abuse
- Murder
- Abuse Against Women

PARISH

Road trips are an American staple. Families and friends pack into a car and see all the wonders that America has to offer. Then there are a select few, which America has more horrors than wonders for. It can be seen throughout history and throughout the present day. There are towns you never want to set foot in. In an era when less books are read much less green, those towns blend into the backdrop of the American landscape. Road trips are an American staple, but some road trips you don't come back from... this is one of those trips.

"Diamond, connect your phone please, cause Pandora got me all the way fucked up," Jada said as she passed the aux cord to the back.

"Your month up already?" Diamond asked.

"Yeah and I'm out of emails to sign-"

"Why she get the cord?" Precious asked.

"What?" Jada replied.

"I'm riding shotgun, why are you passing her the cord? I got a phone," Precious said.

The car grew quiet as Diamond pushed in the cord and started to thumb through her playlist of songs. Diamond kept her eyes on the screen. Brianna continued to ignore the whole car by scanning the nothingness of the road that was passing them by but Imani leaned forward and chose violence.

"Because your music taste is too damn White for this road trip," Imani said.

"Shut up, nobody was talking to you," Precious said.

Imani laughed and kicked at the passenger seat, "Well I'm talking to you, nobody is trying to listen to Taylor Swift for four hours. We're going to the Essence festival not... not... what the fuck do White people go to?"

"Hoe downs," Diamond replied.

"Not no fucking hoe down!" Imani shouted.

"Don't listen to them, baby. I love your music," Jada said as she leaned over for a kiss on the cheek. The car started to swerve as Precious grabbed Jada's chin and turned her lips towards her. Their lips brushed and then locked for only a moment before Brianna leaned forward and put her hand on the wheel straightening the car.

"Come on y'all, Brianna said softly.

Jada looked at the rear view and smiled, "sorry Bri."

Brianna sat back down and stared out the window once again before Diamond selected her song and sat back and let the music of H.E.R fill the car.

"You alright," Diamond asked.

Brianna watched the sun slowly setting over

the town up ahead and she sighed looking back at Diamond, "I'm just in my feelings."

"You have every right to be, I remember when my Grandma died. Shit's hard, Bri," Imani said. She reached over and put her hand on Brianna's leg, "But Mama Williams loved you, and she wouldn't want you locked up in your apartment crying all weekend."

"Imani's right, Bri. Use this weekend to celebrate her, let the world know the love she had for music," Jada laughed and pointed at the rearview mirror, "Remember when she was trying to convince all of us to sign up for her church choir?"

Brianna laughed, "She was done with us when y'all asked if any single men were gonna be there." The whole car got quiet and then they all said in unison, "Church is not where you go to get your kitty pet!"

"She said that?" Precious asked.

"That and 'Don't you go paying no man's bills when you ain't pay the lord his tiehs' Grandma was a trip, that's for sure," Brianna said. She nodded her head for a moment and then looked over at Diamond and Imani, "Y'all are right, I need to get out of my head and just live this weekend for her."

"Yeah, let your... Fuck," Jada rolled her eyes and placed both her hands on the wheel of the car.

"What's wrong?" Precious asked.

"This cop is riding me," Jada said.

"Probably trying to run your plates," Imani said. The car became slight as the women all looked back to see the black and white police cruiser right behind them, close enough that Diamond could make out the driver and his partner as they ran Jada's plate.

"Everybody just be cool," Brianna said.

Precious looked forward and started to dig through her purse, pushing all the mountain of fast food receipts to the side as she searched for the tiny little plastic bag that sat at the bottom of her purse. She pulled it out and proceeded to push the baggy into her underwear. She snapped the purse shut and leaned back, closing her eyes.

"What in the actual fuck, was that?" Jada asked.

"Just in case we-"

"Bitch, what did you just shove in your drawers?" Brianna asked.

"I know your ass didn't bring that shit with you?" Jada said.

"I thought she was clean," Diamond replied.

"You can't clean trash," Imani said.

Precious spun around, "Bitch I've had enough of-"

The red and blue lights mixed with the orange haze of the setting sun and all the hearts in the car stopped at once. Jada slowed the car down and pulled it over to the side, as she did her best to remind herself to keep her hands on the wheel, to smile and to one hundred percent remember to break up with Precious for the final time. Imani pulled out her cell phone and turned it on record, lowering it to rest between her legs, so she could get a good view of the driver side window.

Brianna's hand went out to stop the recording and Imani slapped it away, "Stop playing," Brianna said.

"No one's playing," Imani replied.

"Be cool," Diamond said.

The dirt and gravel crunched under the Officer's black boots as he slowly made his way up to the driver's window, his partner who was only a few short steps behind him, started coming up along the passenger side. The officer on the left stood by the window for a moment before taking his knuckle and knocking into the glass slowly.

Jada rolled down the window with a smile, "Hello officer-"

"License and registration," The officer interrupted.

"Sure, just..." Jada leaned over toward the glove department.

"Slowly," The other officer said.

Jada nodded and opened up the glove department slowly. Her fingers creeped into the mess of napkins and disposable masks, pushing everything aside as Jada internally prayed she had her paperwork.

"Where are you ladies heading? Mighty late for ladies to be driving around alone, the sun's almost down," The officer by the driver window asked.

Jada came back with a folded piece of paper and then pulled her license from her back pocket, "We're not alone, there's five of us," Jada said.

"I mean without a male escort," The officer replied.

Jada leaned in and read the dark engraved letters on the officer's chest, "Well, Officer Bowman. It's not the 40s, women don't need escorts."

"Yeah, we don't need men either," Precious said as she ran her finger up Jada's arm.

Jada pulled her arm away and sighed, "Stop fucking around."

"Watch your mouth," The officer on the right said.

"Is there a reason that you stopped us," Imani asked.

Officer Bowman looked up from the paperwork and right into the lens of Imani's camera before smirking and placing his forearm on the hood of the car, "We stopped you because you were driving without headlights."

"It's daytime," Brianna said.

"According to who's clock?" The officer on the right asked.

"Everyone just chill, listen officer-"

"You don't have any weapons or drugs in the vehicle, do you?" Officer Bowman asked.

"Wow, this is getting really Shaun King, really fast," Imani said.

Officer Bowman looked into the car and smiled, "Can I ask you not to record me."

"Yes you can, I'm still gonna record you, but you can ask me whatever you like," Imani said.

Officer Bowman laughed and nodded, "Good, I'm gonna ask you all to get out of the car."

"Why?" Jada asked.

"Officer Richardson, why are we asking these ladies to exit their vehicle?" Officer Bowman mockingly asked.

"Not only were they driving without headlights, which is extremely dangerous for everyone in our Parish, their car fits the description of a stolen vehicle reported in the neighboring Parish," Officer Richardson said.

"What?" Jada asked.

Officer Bowman smiled and placed his hand on the car door handle, he lifted it slowly, but the lock kept the door in place, "It's gonna be a lot worse if I have to ask again," Officer Bowman said.

"Let's just get out y'all," Diamond said.

Jada sighed and hit the powerlock for the car, the click sounded, freeing all the women from their box of confusion, only for them to be tossed into a space of fear and worry.

"Don't touch me!" Precious shouted and immediately grabbed hold of everyone's attention. Officer Richardson was struggling to get a hold of Precious' arm as pink silk fabric batted and swerved to escape him. He grew tired of the dance and his body came forward, forcing Precious to back up into the car.

"Hey man! Back up off her," Jada shouted.

"Everyone line up on the side of the damn road!" Officer Bowman's hand went back to his waist and another click was heard, this one sent a chill through the women. Jada's eyes locked on the officer and her hands shot up into the air, "I ain't gonna ask y'all again, line up!"

The women all stood still, with their eyes forward, heels trying hard not to follow into the dip on the edge of the road. Officer Richardson dragged Precious past the line of women

"Where are you taking her?" Jada asked.

"Mind your business," Officer Richardson commanded.

"Hey, he can't just be dragging her around like that," Jada shouted.

"Jada, be cool," Diamond said.

"Nah!" Jada shouted.

Officer Bowman's head lifted from looking inside of the driver's side of the car and then he gazed at Officer Richardson for a moment before looking back at the women, "Richardson, line her up with the rest of them."

"She smells funny," Officer Richardson said.

"How you mean," Officer Bowman replied.

"My eyes are burning and they started as soon as she opened her door," Officer Richardson said.

The women looked at one another and Imani clapped her hands, "That's nice, you got red eyes to match your red-"

"Imani!" All the women shouted at once.

"Officer Richardson is allergic to weed and many other drugs, he breaks out into something nasty. He's better than a bloodhound at finding the stuff," Officer Bowman stated. They weren't gonna make it to the Essence Festival, not all of them, not if Officer Richardson started his search. What he would fine, would for sure put and end to Precious' trip, whether or not it put an end to everyone else's trip depending on two things; how much it was gonna cost to get Precious out and if Jada was fucking with her afterwords.

"You can't just be touching on her, you need a female officer," Imani said, she looked over at Officer Richardson and snapped her fingers, "You hear me talking to you, cowboy?"

"They don't have cowboys in Louisiana, do they?" Diamond asked.

"What the fuck ever, he knows I'm right," Imani said.

Officer Bowman sighed and ran his hand over

the back of his neck, "Richardson, put the lady in the back and we'll drive into town. Have Sue look her over."

Officer Richardson nodded then pulled out his handcuffs, "Turn around," he said.

"Does she really need to be handcuffed?" Imani asked.

"You wanna a pair of your own?" Officer Bowman asked.

"I'm good." Imani kept her camera rolling and then she leaned over to whisper in Diamond's ear, "I don't think he likes me."

"Imani, make sure you get their badge numbers and their car number," Brianna said.

Imani nodded and started moving slowly toward Officer Bowman, "Didn't I say to stay lined up?"

"Yeah but I just need to get those-"

"Get on the line!" Officer Richardson shouted after tossing Precious into the back of their patrol car.

Imani quickly ran back to the line and stood with her camera at her hip, "I didn't get the numbers y'all."

Jada stared as the patrol car as Officer Richardson got into the passenger seat and waited on his boss. Officer Bowman started walking over to the women and he sighed, "Sue is gonna check over your friend, if she don't find nothing then you can just pick her up and be on your way," Officer Bowman said.

"What about the stolen car?" Jada asked.

"Oh right, seems we got the model wrong... now if they do find something on her. She's gonna have to post bail or wait to see the Judge on Monday," Officer Bowman said, his hand went out to Jada with all her information and he smiled, "Y'all have a nice night."

Jada looked over at the patrol car as Officer Bowman made his way to it and she called on every last one of the ancestors not to throw a rock and break their damn windshield. The officers closed their doors and just as suddenly as they arrived to turn the ladies world upside down, they were gone and so was Precious. Jada's driver's license bent in her palm as she squeezed her fingers shut. Precious was always getting them into trouble, be it flirting with the wrong person at a bar or getting so drunk she thinks she can fight and Jada has to show her in the nicest of ways that she can't. Precious fucks up a lot, but this one wasn't on Precious, this one wasn't on any of them.

THE WOMEN GOT BACK into the car and Imani turned her recording off, "They stopped us cause we're Black," Imani said.

"Yep," Diamond replied.

"We need to send that video to-"

"Only thing we need to do is go pick up Precious," Jada said. Her voice was low and cold, she didn't want to argue with anyone, she didn't want to take on the fight of the Black community, all she wanted to do was get her girlfriend and get to the hotel.

"We got to stop at the bank first," Brianna said. Everyone's eyes turned in her direction and she shrugged, "Unless you think Officer Redneck takes Cash App."

A storm of tan dirt and pebbles sprayed through the air as the tires sped back onto the black top. The police car wasn't too far ahead of them, so they followed them down the highway, passing signs for rest stops and fast food, passing exit after exit. All the while they argued about what was the best way to handle everything. They were unjustly stopped, was the clear topic but whether or not it was worth fighting was the narrative that they were finding hard to lockdown. As their tires turned right to follow the police car off the exit, they watched as all the comforts they were used to slowly slipped away. The streets were dark now and the roads became smaller, until there were no lines on the roads and then there was no road. Just dirt that was kicking up on the windshield.

"Where the hell are we?" Brianna asked from the passenger seat. She leaned in to see if she could peep through the dirt for some signs of life, "Turn the wipers on."

"Anyone got any service?" Diamond asked.

"Nah," The car said in unison.

As the dirt cleared away from the windshield, Jada sighed and slowed to a stop, "Where the cop car go?"

"We have to stop at an ATM anyways, we'll just ask where the police station is while we get the cash," Brianna said.

"I don't even wanna get out of the car, much less ask for directions," Imani said. Her finger hit the automatic lock on her door as she stared at the rundown post office and the red and blue fabric that danced in the cool breeze of the summer night, "They got confederate flags at the post office, y'all."

"That's illegal," Diamond said.

"Yeah maybe in America, we are in Amerikkka, with the three Ks," Imani said, she leaned forward and looked at Brianna and then looked at Jada, "So I've been thinking."

"If what you're thinking about involves leaving Precious, just keep it to yourself," Jada said.

Imani rolled her eyes and looked back at Brianna, "Bri, I've been thinking... none of us even like Precious-"

"Imani! I'm not playing with you!" Jada shouted.

"Ain't nobody playing with you. Bitch ain't nobody trying to time travel to the 1920s so you can get some stank ass drug addict coochie," Imani replied.

With that statement, Jada slammed her foot on the gas and took off down the street. Brianna's hands slapped onto the dashboard as she watched run down building after rundown building whip past them. Diamond wrapped her arms around Imani and pulled her back into her seat, once she did that the car started to slow down.

"Oh you lucky, cause I was about to let your ass fly through this windshield, keep playing with me," Jada said.

"You need help, maybe from a mental hospital and then follow that shit up with Jesus," Imani said.

The car slowly pulled into a dimly lit gas station that had two old pumps sitting in the middle of a large slab of concert. Jada pulled the car up to the pump and sighed as she rested her head back on the seat, "How much money do you need us to chip in?" Jada asked.

"Chip in? Us? What language is she speaking?" Imani asked.

Brianna leaned down and opened up her Freddy backpack, "It's alright I got it," she said as she pulled out her elm street purse, "Let's go free your jailbird."

"You got Freddy's nails too, hoe?" Jade asked with a laugh.

"Oh, I guess you'll be paying for-"

"I'm just playing! I'm sorry, I mean it's nice, just creepy-"

Jada jumped when her window shook under the balled up dirty fist of the gas station attendant, "Y'all lost?" He shouted.

Jada turned and let the window down a crack and smiled, "Yes and no, we were hoping you had an ATM inside that we could use and maybe you knew where the police station is?" Jada asked.

The old man laughed and rested his arm on the hood of the car, stale sweat and cheap whiskey caused Jada to close her eyes and discreetly place her finger under her nose, "We ain't got no ATM but I know where the police station is, I'm there every weekend."

"Oh, are you a volunteer officer?" Brianna asked.

"No ma'am, I'm a drunk." The old man smiled and the car broke out into laughter, "Y'all are gonna keep going down this road and make two rights and a left, you can't miss it," The old man said.

"Thank you, sir," Jada replied.

"Y'all be careful now, it's late and the town ain't as nice as it used to be," The old man said and then he turned walking back to the flicking lights of the gas station.

"What do you think he means by that?" Brianna asked.

The car grew silent as they all thought about the odd warning, the town seemed to be trapped in its past and from the sight of the old dixie flags that hung limply from every other building, it was a past that no one in the car would label as 'nice' Brianna's eyes scanned the homes and buildings as they made their way down the street, every now and then she saw faces, masked by white curtains or shadows, keeping them from being human in Brianna's eyes, just figures watching them from the darkness.

"What do we do about bail?" Imani asked.

"I thought you weren't helping?" Jada said as she looked at Imani through the mirror. The women smiled at one another and Jada wondered why she always let Imani get under her skin. Why couldn't she just hear her words and overlook them like everyone else's. Their eyes must have lingered too long because Imani turned and stared out the window along with Brianna.

"These people don't believe in street lights?" Imani asked.

"What's out there worth lighting up?" Diamond asked.

"Cold blooded," Jada said.

"What? It's true, it looks like one of those abandoned towns from Brianna's horror movies," Diamond replied.

Brianna pulled out her phone and sighed at the flat line that replaced the five bars she normally saw when she was in civilization. They came to a stop in a faded parking spot and Jada pushed the black button killing the engine before pushing her car door open.

"Someone come with me," Jada said.

"Umm-"

Diamond was cut off by Brianna's car door flying open, "We're all going."

"Thank you, Bri," Jada said.

"Yeah, thanks Bri," Imani and Diamond said as they stuck their tongues out at Brianna. For a moment they looked like they did the first time Brianna saw them, five years old in matching pigtail braids. Two friends who wanted to be twins so badly, never seeing one without the other. Brianna was alway a bit jealous of that kind of friendship, the kind that was more like a sisterhood than just a friend, but then they all accepted her into their little family.

"Eww," Diamond squealed. She dragged her white air forces along the first step to the police station, "something sticky is on the floor."

They all followed behind Jada, ignoring Diamond's words, marching into the brightly lit police station looking for a fight and only seeing an empty waiting area. Diamond's foot dragged onto the faded tiles of the station, and revealed a dark red streak. Diamond stared down at the streak and then picked her foot up from the floor. Her white soles were now stained red.

"Hello?" Jada said softly.

"Maybe the hot light is on at Krispy Kreme," Imani joked.

"Guys..." Diamond looked up at their backs and through the gaps of her friends she could see dark dots leading deeper into the police station, "I think it's blood."

"What's blood-"

Before their eyes could turn to Diamond's wide glare, their attention was pulled forward by the chilling country shriek of an older white woman, "Hey! What are y'all doing here? Visiting hours are over!" Jada always had to remind herself when she was talking to older people that they were someone's parent or grandparent, and that respect should be given on that alone, but as the woman slammed her hand on the table, "Get out!" Respect quickly got left at the door.

"Ain't nobody coming here to visit! I'm here to get my girlfriend." Jada's tone gave off a 'test me if you want to' vibe, which Brianna knew was not going to do anything besides get them all locked up for the weekend, her hand grabbed hold of Jada's hand and pulled her back.

"Relax," Brianna whispered.

Imani pulled out her phone once again and tapped the record button. She really wished she could have been live streaming the whole thing to her followers, but they hadn't had service for most of the day traveling to the festival, "And here we have the second act, introducing a new character... I'm gonna call her Officer Karen."

"No recording!" The old woman shouted, she quickly started to wobble from around the counter and Brianna stepped in between her friends and the woman.

"Listen, our friend was brought in a little while ago, we just came to bail her out," Brianna said.

"No one was brought in today," The older woman said.

Diamond came forward with her shoe turned upside down in her hand, "There's blood on the floor."

Silence, all that could be heard was the dull humming of the overhead lights that transformed those dark spots from dirt into something far more wicked. Just the humming of the lights that transformed a rude little old lady and twisted her into something far worse.

"It's time for you to leav-" The old woman didn't get to finish her statement as Jada's open palm muffed the left side of the woman's face, pushing her back into the old counter of the police station. Jada took off down the hallway, following the dark spots deeper into the heart of the station. The rest of the crew followed behind her.

"You can't go back there!" The woman shouted behind them. Brianna could hear her little legs forcing her flat feet into the floor as she chased them down the hall. Over Brianna's shoulder was Imani racing with her phone held tightly in her hand. The video picking up blurs and voices. Behind her was Diamond with her one shoe in her hand, running, only running because she wasn't sure what to do with herself. Putting her shoe back on seemed wrong in her head. Stopping and talking to that women seemed stupid, so she ran and she ran until Diamond and everyone else collided with Jada who was stone still. Eyes fixated on the blood pouring out from under the white sheet.

"What are y'all doing back here? Susan!" Officer Bowman hollered.

They didn't want it to be seen. Susan was to stand guard at the door but something pulled her mind away from that task, maybe she wanted to clean the blood trail that they left. Maybe she didn't think there was anything worth hiding. You only keep something a secret if you know it's wrong. Maybe this wasn't wrong to her. Whatever it was going through any of their heads, the girls weren't meant to see this. The white sheet that covered Precious' body had soaked up her blood and clung to her like a horrific red veil.

"Precious!" Jada's body gave way to the scream, it relocated all of its energy to her voice, to her cry. Her knees buckled. Her eyes closed and her body crumbled into Brianna's arms, "Precious!"

Brianna's arms hugged Jada's body to her own, "What the fuck did you do!"

"The suspect-"

"Suspect!" Imani shoved her phone into the face of Officer Bowman, "She ain't no fucking suspect!"

"Give me that damn phone," Imani's hand pulled back as Officer Bowman's hands reached out, Diamond got an unwanted elbow to the nose in the process causing her to fall back into Susan's arms.

"Sonny!" Susan's voice echoed down the hall and out of the darkness of a supply closet came Officer Richardson with a shovel over his shoulder. He swung the shovel down until the metal slammed into the tile floor, letting off a loud crack as it connected, "We can't let 'em leave."

Imani didn't hear Susan's orders because she already took off down the hallway. She was not one to ask questions and talk when things got physical. No Imani can be counted on to do one of two things. Throw hands or run track and as her feet slid through Precious' blood, it was clear she was in track mode. Her left foot hit the parking lot and slipped out from under her. Imani's hands hit the ground before her face, saving her a lot of pain and a lot of sad selfie shots.

"Fuck!" Imani shouted.

Imani felt arms grab hold of her, and turned to let her fist fly only to see Jada dragging her to her feet, "Move!" The car beeped and its engine came to life as Jada unlocked the doors. Diamond raced past them and ripped the door to the backseat open, she jumped in with her one shoe, the other was sacrificed as Diamond used it to beat her way free of Susan's boney hold. It felt like a grandmother's death grip, being locked around her waist, her hips ached from the old bones pushing into her.

"Let's go!" Diamond shouted and the rest of the girls loaded up into the car. Brianna jumped into the back seat with Diamond. Jada and Imani both went in through the driver's side, Imani quickly crawling into the passenger seat. The doors went flying wildly as Jada tossed the car into reverse. Diamond watched the police station doors blast open as Officer Richardson came sprinting toward the car, "Go, go, go!"

The shovel came swinging as the back tires hit the curb of the parking lot and started to go onto the sidewalk. Glass shattered as the metal crashed through the windshield. Richardson pulled back on the shovel and ripped a chunk of the windshield free from the car. Jada's foot was pressed down to the floor of the car but the car was still. Jada's head poked free from her open door to see the car had jumped the curb but not the large stone that was placed on the sidewalk, most likely placed there by Officer Bowman to stop curb jumpers. The shovel came crashing down into the windshield once again, this time sending glass flying into the car and peppering Jada and Imani.

"Car's stuck!" Jada shouted before jumping free from the car. Imani pushed her door open and took off running into the darkness of the street. Brianna pushed her door open only to watch it slam into the sidewalk. She jumped free from the car and took off down the road, side by side with Jada as they raced through the darkness behind Imani.

"Imani!" The scream caused all the running to stop and it caused Imani's eyes to turn from the darkness of the street back toward the lights of the parking lot. Imani knew that scream and that tone. It only happened two other times during their friendship, once when a dog broke free from its yard and cornered that scream in an alley. The second time was when the drinks were too sweet and things got dizzy and then found that scream was cornered in some random boy's bedroom. It was Diamond's scream, the one she saved for when she thought her life was in danger, the one she used for the only person she always thought would save her.

"Diamond!" Imani went racing back toward her lifelong friend only to feel the arms of more friends keeping her at bay. Richardson had a handful of Diamond's black braids, he pulled her back until her eyes were focused on the stars above. Her chest rose and fell as her heart pounded in her chest. The cool night air kissed her skin as her head slammed back into the asphalt. Diamond stared up at the stars and while she couldn't hear Imani's screams, she knew she was near and that she hadn't left her alone.

"Fucking bitch!" The shovel ripped through the skin and flesh until it cracked her cheek bone, "Dumb, fucking, bitch!" The shovel rose again and came down slicing through Diamond's skull. Braids and blood skated along the blacktop as Imani's screams filled the streets. Richardson looked up from his bloody shovel and then smiled as he pointed it toward the girls, "Look what y'all made me do!"

Dragging Imani away would have been damn near impossible if it wasn't for Officer Bowman stepping into the street, pointing his gun. The sight of the black metal put everything back into perspective. Imani remembered what she was doing before Richardson ripped her world apart, she was running and that's what she continued to do, deeper into the darkness of the street.

"Son of a bitch!" Officer Bowman shouted.

"I didn't hear them walk in-"

"Shut up, Susan! Let me think." Officer Bowman ran the barrel of his revolver along the side of his head, tapping the base of his tan cowboy hat with every rub, "We can't let those girls leave, not with that recording."

"I can get in the truck... hunt em' down," Officer Richardson said. Reached into his back pocket and pulled out a green tin. Richardson gave it a hard shake between his fingers before popping the top and grabbing a pitch of black dip and pushing it between his lip and teeth, "They shouldn't be too hard to find."

Officer Bowman stared down at the lifeless body at Officer Richardson's feet. The blood had quickly taken over the road. Officer Bowman sighed and then looked back at the building, the bodies were stacking up. What could have been a nice story of self defense got shitted on when Richardson shot the first girl in the back and now there was one bleeding out on the street with half her head gone. There was no way of writing this one off and putting a nice bow on it. They murdered these girls and now they needed to murder the rest.

"Don't you think you've done enough?" Officer Bowman said without even looking back at Richardson.

"Don't be like that, boss." Richardson said.

"He didn't mean no harm, it was those damn girls. Got him all heated up, he wasn't thinking straight," Susan said.

Officer Bowman pitched the bone between his eyes and sighed, "We'll split up, cover more ground that way. Susan, you stay here and clean this mess up." Officer Bowman motioned at the body and then shoved his weapon back into its holster.

Susan nodded and started back toward the police station, Richardson smiled as he watched his Mama wobble through the parking lot and then he looked at Officer Bowman, when she was out of ear shot, "When we find them, do you think I could have one? Just for a little while?"

Officer Bowman looked over at Richardson and then turned his back walking off toward his car, "Stop thinking with dick and go find those damn girls."

JADA'S CHEST burned like cheese grater was rubbing continuously into her skin, just scratching away the outer layer of flesh. The same feeling started to spread from her inner thigh to her calves. When they started Jada could see Imani and could hear Brianna breathing beside her, but now she could barely make out Imani in the darkness ahead and the only breathing she could hear was her own. No one ever really thinks about how much they should be running daily until they see how poorly they run in real time. Jada always made that joke, that she would only run if something was chasing her, but who knew that something would be an evil racist hillbilly with a badge. Jada's body was slowly giving out on her. Her strade got shorter and shorter until she realized she wasn't running anymore. She was just staring at the ground, trying to pull air back into her lungs.

"Jada!" Brianna hissed from up ahead, "Imani!"

Brianna began her jog back to her friend, looking for any signs of the horrors that they left behind. The lights of the police station were long gone, lost to the many turns and backyards that the trio had cut through as they ran for their lives.

"Shit," Jada said softly as she looked back into the darkness of the road, "I think we lost them."

"Maybe, but we have to keep going," Brianna said.

"Keep going where?" Jada asked.

"Anywhere other than here," Imani said. The girls' eyes found her looking into an empty yard from a chained fence, "We gotta get out of here."

"We got to get help," Brianna said.

"From who?" Imani turned around and stared at the two and then clapped her hands to get their attention, "From who?"

"I don't know, anyone," Brianna said.

"Yeah, let's just tell the locals their police officers just killed our friends and now they're after us-"

"Oh God, what the fucking is happening," Jada screamed.

Brianna's hand went over Jada's lips and she shook her head, "No, not now... we need to keep it together."

Jada pulled Brianna's hand down, "My girlfriend was just-"

"Diamond died too," Imani quickly interrupted, "But all you care about is your trashy ass, booty call."

"You dumb bit-"

"Stop it!" Brianna hissed, "Stop it, right now... we're all hurt, there's no need to hurt each other even more." Brianna kept her eyes on the direction that they came, "We need help and we need to get off the streets."

"We don't need help, we need a ride out of this place," Imani turned back to the fence and pointed at the flickering lights through the night's darkness, "And I know where to find one."

"What's that?" Jada asked.

"I think it's that gas station," Brianna said.

"That old man has a truck parked on the side, I say we borrow his truck and-"

"So your plan to avoid cops that are chasing us is to commit a crime?" Jada asked.

"I mean if you want we can ask first? But after he shoots you, I'm taking the truck," Imani said.

Brianna's eyes turned back to the road and the distant glow that was growing on it, "Whatever we're doing, lets do it now." Brianna said as she ran toward the fence and hopped over it into the tall grass of the yard and then took off running for the next fence. Jada and Imani quickly followed behind her.

RICHARDSON TOOK the right turn slowly, with his headlights scanning all the little dark pockets of the town. The glow overtook the water damaged siding of most of the houses, the chipped light blue paint that covered all their pouches. Every morning he woke up half hung over with the same thought in his mind 'I shouldn't be here' because Richardson was created for great things, or that's what he told himself every time he put that uniform on.

Richardson looked down at the blood stains that painted his only clean pair of pants. He licked his thumb and began to run it down the dark splash that Diamond had left behind on the fabric.

The car radio crackled for a moment and then Officer Bowman's voices came blaring out of the radio, "Richardson! I swear to fucking God!"

Richardson's hand shot up from his lap and he grabbed the receiver. He looked around to see if Bowman was nearby, watching him, waiting for him to mess up. Richardson held down the button on the receiver and then licked the blood off his thumb, "What you hollering about, boss?"

"Your damn Mama is on the town radio!" Officer Bowman shouted.

Richardson clicked off the office radio and mashed the button for the town radio. The town wasn't what it used to be. The highway had pretty much bypassed it, making it forgotten by the rest of the state. Just a lost memory of what America used to be. People left, abandoned the dying streets before its ghosts could reach up from the graves and drag them down. But those that stayed, all got little CB radios, to make communication easier.

"Susan, why are you playing on that radio?"

"No one is playing, Bobby Jean, there are three armed suspects running around town," Susan said.

"Oh my God!"

"What do they look like?"

"They look like they weren't born here, Julie, use your head," Bobby Jean said.

"They're three Black women-

"Oooh."

"I'm gonna get my truck and help-"

Richardson clicked the radio back to the office channel only to hear Officer Bowman's voice booming through the speakers, "She's gonna start a fucking mob!"

"Maybe that's what we need, all hands on deck," Richardson said.

"The less people that know about this the better," Officer Bowman said.

"No one in town is gonna care about these girls ," Richardson replied.

"For your sake I hope not, because I'm not the one going to prison because he caught a case of jungle fever..." The line went dead for a moment and then Officer Bowman laughed, "I think I just spotted them hopping a fence. Meet me on Jefferson street."

With that the radio went silent, Richardson licked his thumb again and started dragging it along the fabric, his eyes focused on his pants as Mr. Johnson and his son Ricky went speeding down the street in their pick up truck.

"It's hunting season!" Ricky shouted as he leaned out of the passenger window.

Richardson looked up and smiled and then followed behind the pair.

IMANI DROPPED down over the last fence and stared at the flickering light of the gas station, before watching as Jada's boots came over the wooden fence. They dangled there for a moment, fearful of what was to come. The fall, Jada was always afraid of the fall and more importantly the unknown.

That's why she kept going back to a broken relationship, that's why she didn't take those jobs out of state and that's why her and Imani were still just friends, because of the fear of the unknown and the fall.

"Just let go," Imani said softly.

Jada looked over her shoulder and dropped down two feet before her boots smacked into the sidewalk. Brianna looked over at the gas station and sighed, "You think he's still there?"

"The truck's still there, that's all that matters," Imani said.

The girls quickly made their way across the street and toward the blinking lights of the gas station. There was no movement inside from what Brianna could see and there was no sign of life on the street other than their own as Jada followed behind Imani who was creeping up to the driver side door of the truck.

Imani pulled the door handle and the door popped open, "Jackpot."

The girl's loaded up into the truck and slammed the doors behind them, "Let's get the hell out of here," Brianna said.

Imani started pulling at the sun visors and then leaned over to open the glove compartment, "What are you doing?" Jada asked.

"Looking for the keys," Imani said.

"You can't hotwire it?" Brianna asked.

Imani stopped cold and leaned back to get a clear look at Brianna, "Bitch, how long have you known me? You ever seen me hotwire a fucking car?"

"No, but you seemed so sure about stealing the

car, I just thought you had a plan!" Brianna hissed back.

"Move," Jada said as she tossed her leg over Imani, straddling her in the driver's seat. Their eyes locked as Jada pushed the driver door open, and then crawled out of the truck.

"Where you going?" Imani asked.

"I'm gonna see if that old man-"

"There they are, Daddy!" Ricky shouted, his father slammed down on the brakes causing Rick to slam his ribs into the window frame, something that would have ruined the night, if his father and him weren't half a bottle deep into their spiced rum before they decided to go out and 'save the town' as Mr. Johnson put it. Ricky leaned into the truck and pulled out his shotgun. The boy... no he was running into a battle with a weapon, looking to end someone's life. No, Ricky wasn't a boy but a man who held that shotgun up into the air as he laughed, "There they are!" The truck jumped the curb and came into the gas station parking lot. Jada took off running toward the entrance to the gas station. When her hand pulled on the door the bell sounded and right after that a loud blast blew out the glass of the shop door. The shards peppered Jada's back as she raced into the shop, "Damn!"

"You missed!" Mr. Johnson broke out laughing.

"It's because the truck was moving," Rick argued. He popped open the shotgun and stared at Imani and Brianna who were standing by the truck, "Don't worry..." the empty shells hit the floor and Ricky held up two new rounds, "We got more."

"Move!" Brianna shouted. Imani and Brianna took off racing toward the shop door. Glass cracked under their shoes as they pushed into the gas station. Imani's eyes locked with the old man behind the counter, he put his finger to his lip and then pointed toward the back of the shop. Imani and Brianna continued moving deeper into the gas station before Jada popped her head out of the bathroom door.

"In here," Jada said. They all piled into the bathroom and closed the door behind them, quickly locking it.

Ricky came racing into the gas station with his shotgun at the ready, "Where you bitches at!"

"Ricky..." the old man said softly before picking up a paper cup and spitting a stream of black liquid into the cup, "You shot out my window boy."

"Where those girls go?" Ricky asked, his head poked up as he got on his tippy toes to see over the racks of chips.

The old man's hand slowly went down below the counter, right next to his handgun. His fingers wrapped around the handle, "Now I'm gonna have to close the shop down while I get that fixed," The old man said.

"You ain't hear Susan on the radio?" Ricky asked.

"I make it my life's mission not to hear that hippo's voice, why?" The old man asked.

"There are three little armed hood rats on the loose and they ran in here," Ricky looked around the shop as he father took his first steps onto the broken glass.

"Did these girls come in before or after you shot out my window?" The old man asked.

"Now, Cash... I don't think you understand-"

The old man's eyes went to Ricky's father when he said his name. Cash smiled and pulled back the hammer on his gun, "I don't think you understand, Mr. Johnson. This shop has been in my family since before you were a shot in the pussy that your mother should have swallowed."

"Now listen here!" Mr. Johnson shouted.

"I got my gun on your boy, Mr. Johnson." Ricky started to turn toward the old man, with his shotgun held firmly in his hands, "Son, if you're gonna make any movement, it better be out that damn door you shot up, because I'll put one in your belly button and sleep like a baby while you scream."

The Johnsons stared at one another and then Ricky shook his head, "I'm gonna tell the Sheriff about this."

"Good, you can tell him I took your guns too... drop em'" Cash said.

"Now-"

"Toss the damn guns on the floor and get the hell out!" Cash shouted and without any other complaints, the shotguns were tossed on the floor and the Johnsons slowly backed up over the broken glass and outside of the store. Cash stood still at the counter only turning his head to watch them walk back to their truck. When they loaded up and pulled off Cash let out a breath, "They're gone!"

The trio stood still behind the bathroom door and then Brianna's hand went for the door handle, "What are you doing?" Imani asked.

"If he wanted to hurt us, he wouldn't have let us in here," Brianna pushed the door open to see Cash standing in front of them, staring with his revolver held firmly in his hand.

"Y'all ever find that ATM? Cause someone owes me a new shop door," Cash said.

Imani pushed through the doorway, "We need your truck."

"There's people after us," Brianna said.

"I'm not too bright but when the people after you are the cops, that normally means you did something," Cash said.

"Not in this backward ass town," Jada said. She folded her arms over her chest and then stared at the entrance to the shop, "They killed our friends."

"Who?" Cash asked.

"Those fucking psycho cops and now they're after us... so like I said, we need your truck," Imani said.

"Richardson and Bowman? They killed your friends? I ain't never seen Bowman kill a deer, much less a person... Richardson, now that boy's a psychopath if I ever did see one," Cash said, "Radio said you're armed and dangerous, are you?"

"Do we look it?" Brianna asked.

"No and that's too bad, because that's what y'all are gonna need to be to get out of this," Cash said. He released the hammer on his gun and closed the bathroom door behind them, "This town... well it wasn't nice to begin with and then it just got worse, it's not a place for girls like you."

"What? Black girls?" Imani asked.

"Yes, think of it like this... time forgot this place and all the country ass people in it. They keep living, breeding, going through the motions but ain't nothing change for them, everything is just the outside world. Kind of like a tv show in the background, you hear it, maybe even look at it but it ain't changing what you got going on in your life," Cash said.

"That's a deep ass excuse for racism, can we have the keys now?" Imani said and was met with an elbow to her side.

Cash stared at Imani for a moment and then turned around and started walking back to the counter. He pulled up his stool and sat down letting out a soft sigh before he reached over and grabbed his keys, "Here."

"That's it, you believe us?" Brianna asked.

"Whether you're lying or telling the truth, I'm just gonna report it stolen to the insurance company anyway. Get me one of those nice Teslas," Cash said with a smile, he thumbed through his keys and then pulled one off the ring, "Besides, this town ain't kind to outsiders. If you did something, it's best you pay for it outside of here." Cash looked up at the girls and smiled for a moment before placing the key on the counter.

"So you're the only non-racist living in a town of racist?" Imani asked.

"Don't know what to tell you, darling. Born here, the military sent me elsewhere, broke me and I came back home to die…" Cash tapped his finger on the table and smiled, "There's a lot of details in between all that, but maybe I'll tell y'all some other time."

Imani grabbed the key off the counter and nodded, "Maybe."

Red and blue lights started to fill up the shop window and Cash leaned over the lottery tickets to see Richardson and Bowman making their way toward the shop, "Y'all might want to get back in the bathroom, while I deal with this," Cash said. There was no need for a second warning. The girls quickly raced back into the bathroom. As the door closed Imani rested her head on the wall and internally screamed for not grabbing one of the shotguns those hillbillies left on the floor.

"What a mess!" Richardson said as he stepped through the broken shop door, glass cracked under his heel and he smiled as he looked at Cash, "You get drunk and shoot out your window, Cash?"

Cash smiled and kept his revolver below the counter in his hand, "I was just about to call y'all, The Johnson boy came up here, shooting his shotgun and smelling like cheap rum. Boy took out my door. I had to scare him and his drunk Daddy off."

Bowman looked around the shop and then leaned down picking up the pair of shotguns off the floor, "That's funny, because the Johnsons said that our suspects ran up in here and you stopped them from getting them out," Bowman passed a shotgun to Richardson, who smiled as he popped it open to check if it was loaded, "That wouldn't be true would it, Cash? You wouldn't be aiding and abetting criminals now are you?"

Cash's fingers tightened around the revolver handle and his thumb rested on the hammer, "I ain't seen nobody but those drunks all night."

"Then you wouldn't mind if we took a look around would you?" Officer Bowman asked.

"You got a warrant?" Cash asked.

"It's a public gas station, Cash," Richardson said.

"We're closed for cleaning," Cash said as he motioned toward the glass.

Officer Bowman stared at the glass and held the shotgun firmly in his hands, "You know when you came back here, with your little wife, everyone wanted to run you out of town, but I said leave him be."

"I'm gonna tell you right now, things will not end well, if we start talking about my wife," Cash said.

Richardson laughed, "Oh right, you came back with one of them dark girls after the war, right? What was that like? I've been trying to find out." The hammer pulled back on Cash's revolver and Richardson smiled, backing up with his hands in the air, "I was just making conversation."

"You wanna know what it's like Richardson? Half the town could tell you, ain't that right, Cash?" Officer Bowman said. He looked around the room and smiled, "Whole town showed up one night to find out what she felt like."

The revolver came out from its hiding spot and aimed for the middle of Officer Bowman's head, "If you and that shit stained mama's boy wanna keep breathing air outside of a graveyard then I suggest you leave," Cash said.

Officer Bowman stared down the barrel of Cash's 45' for a moment before turning toward the broken door, "Come on Richardson, you heard the man."

Richardson smiled and tipped his hat at Cash before following Officer Bowman out of the shop.

Cash stood there with the revolver still pointed out, his arm stiff as his body tried to fight back the thoughts of that night. The night Cash brought someone he loved home, only to find out he grew up in hell. The revolver came down and Cash put his hands over his face, trying to force the tears back.

"On second thought!" Officer Bowman came in with the shotgun aimed, Cash's hands dropped quickly going for the revolver only to be cut short by the blast of the shotgun. The old man's body lifted off the ground and slammed into the rack of cigarettes, his blood painting all the white packs a dark red, "I've been dying to shut your drunk ass up since we put your whore in that box."

"Damn boss! Why didn't you let me shoot him?" Richardson asked.

"I ain't shot nobody, those little thugs did, came in and robbed the poor bastard. They've been turning our town upside down," Officer Bowman said as he walked past Richardson and started to make his way deeper into the shop.

After hearing that shotgun go off the trio had to call on everything within them not to scream, Imani held onto Brianna's heels as she pushed open the bathroom window and started to climb out. Imani helped her the last of the way and then she turned to look at Jada, she pointed at Jada, letting her know she was next and Jada shook her head.

"Y'all might as well come out now and give me

that cell phone, because the longer I have to wait, the worse it's gonna be for you!" Bowman shouted.

Jada's eyes were focused on the door and when she turned around, she was face to face with Imani, who did something that Jada had been praying for and actively avoiding her whole life. Imani kissed her, and held her lips softly between her own. Imani's shaky hands rested on the back of Jada's neck as she kissed her deeply, for what felt like the first and last time all at once. Imani stepped back and then cupped her hands at the base of the window, she stared at Jada and nodded. Jada stepped into Imani's hand and was pushed up and through the window, only to meet Brianna who helped her down on the other side.

"Imani! Come on," Brianna hissed.

Imani's boot went on the toilet, she lifted herself up till her fingers could brush the edge of the window. She placed her other foot on the trash can. A desperate balancing act was all that separated Imani from a fate like Diamond's. Her fingers dug into the metal frame of the window.

"I'll check the cooler, you go and check the bathroom," Officer Bowman said.

Richardson nodded and slowly creeped over to the bathroom door, he twisted the door handle, but it didn't move, "Got ya," Richardson said. He took a step back and pumped the shotgun before pulling the trigger and blasting a hole where the handle once stood. Richardson ripped open the door, only to find the metal from the door handle scattered throughout the bathroom and peppered holes throughout the tiled walls from where the rounds found their mark. Richardson looked up at the window and then sighed, "Boss!"

The engine roared to life after Imani's trembling fingers finally pushed the key into its slot. The truck frantically backed out, slamming into the patrol car and forcing it over into another parking spot before pulling out of the gas station. Brianna could see the officers running after them in the street. The shotgun blasts filled the night air and Brianna ducked down with each shot, but the shots couldn't reach far enough, Cash's old beat up truck won its fight against the law for the first time.

"Thank God!" Brianna shouted, "Lets get the hell out of here." She looked over at the duo who were keeping their eyes glued to the road, "Y'all alright?"

Jada quickly turned and started hitting Imani, "What the hell is wrong with you! What did you do that for?"

"Stop it!" Imani shouted and then looked over at Jada, the two stared at each other for a moment and Imani bit down on her lip, "What if I died? Like what if I died and you never knew?"

"What if you did? Then I would have had to live with that, that's not fair," Jada said.

"Am I missing something," Brianna asked.

"No, you're-" The truck came to a rolling stop as the headlights shined on a group of people all standing in the road. There were old men and women, people Brianna's age and younger, all standing there, blocking off the road. Imani slowly backed up the truck and turned back down the road toward the police station.

"What was that?" Jada asked.

"That was some Children of The Corn shit," Brianna said.

The truck slowed down again but this time it was just Susan standing in the middle of the dark road, the headlights blinding her as she smiled at the girls, "What's she doing?" Jada asked.

"All she's doing is pissing me the hell off," Imani said, she looked at the girls and they all nodded. Imani's foot slammed down on the gas and the truck came speeding down the road. Jada took hold of Brianna's hand and then placed her hand on Imani's thigh as the truck raced toward a smiling Susan, "You stupid bitch!" they are shouted in unison, they were waiting for that satisfying sound of Susan's body breaking under the front tire and then bouncing between the road and the underbelly of the truck before the back tires fused her skin with the asphalt, but they didn't get that sound, what they got when they were just five feet away from Susan was two loud pops and two more. Imani's fingers tightened around the wheel as she tried fighting against the force of the truck going rogue. The front tires hit the curb and the truck flipped through the air. Susan watched as the metal tossed through the cool night air like a large firefly as the headlights twisted and turned in the air before finally crashing down into the middle of the station's parking lot.

Susan leaned over and grabbed the shovel that still had Diamond's blood on it, but not it was caked with fresh dirt. She dragged it down the road and then started to pull in the road spikes. Susan tossed the spikes on the sidewalk as she watched the crowd of people, slowly making their way down toward the police station. Susan wobbled back and forth toward the truck. She came up on the passenger's side and saw Brianna's unblinking eyes staring back at her. Brianna's whole body was sitting on top of her neck. Susan smiled and slowly started wobbling to the driver's side, she leaned down with the shovel bracing her, as she stared in to see Imani flat on her back.

"Should of wore your seatbelt you dumb bit-" Imani's boot went flying forward and slammed into Susan's face, crumbling the old cartilage that held her nose together. The old woman stumbled back screaming into the night air as the blood began to rush from her nose. Imani's hands slapped into the metal of the doorframe, dragging herself free from the broken glass. When Imani stood up it was just in time to see a shovel come swinging at her head.

Imani shot forward and grabbed the handle of the shovel, "Give me that, you psycho." The two struggled over the shovel until Imani rammed the handle forward, jabbing the wood into Susan's throat. The old woman released the shovel and felt the metal slam into her head. Susan's body crumbled to the ground like a lifeless ragdoll.

"Brianna!" Jada screamed, "No, no, no." Jada tried to pull her friend free from the twisted metal of the crash, but there was no use. Brianna's body was blocked by the dashboard that caved in on her legs, while her body folded in on her neck.

Imani grabbed Jada, pulling her from the truck, "We need to go!"

"Go where," Jada asked.

Imani looked down at Susan and then she quickly dragged the woman to her feet, putting the shovel handle across her throat as she held Susan up. The crowd of people were descending on the parking lot as Imani and Jada started backing up toward the doors of the police station with their new hostage.

"They got Susan!"

"Call Officer Richardson, tell em' those whores got his Mama!"

The crowd was turning into a mob, watching one of their own being dragged into the police station. Jada locked the doors, but one good brick could put an end to any hiding. The people surrounded the front, their fist slamming into the glass, their lips spewing hate and death threats as far as their lungs would allow.

"What now?" Jada asked.

"Just help me get her to the back," Imani said. Jada grabbed Susan by one hand, while Imani held the other and dragged the woman out of sight of the crowd.

The glass began to shake under pounding fists. The shouting of the mob could be heard for miles, it's what caused Officer Bowman and Richardson to return to the police station, that and the smoke from the truck. Richardson stared at Brianna's body and sighed, "What a waste, she was a cute one."

"What did I say?" Officer Bowman asked.

"Stop thinking with my dick," Richardson replied. The two officers slowly made their way toward the mob banging on the station door. Officer Bowman pulled out his handgun and fired a round into the air. The screaming and fist pounding stopped, the shot grabbed the mob's attention.

"What the hell is going on here?" Office Bowman asked.

"Those girls took Susan hostage, dragged her into the station," One woman said.

Richardson stepped forward and pumped his shotgun, "They got my Mama in there?" Richardson started pulling on the locked door, then he took a step back and aimed the shotgun at the glass.

"I wouldn't do that if I were you, Mama's boy." The voice pushed free from Richardson and Officer Bowman's hips. The crackling started as Richardson stepped back from the glass, "Anyone comes in here or tries anything we don't like and I'll put an extra hole in her head," Imani said as she released the button on the radio.

Officer Bowman pulled out his radio and laughed, "Nice bluff, sweetie, but y'all ain't got no weapons."

Imani held down the button and smiled, "I got a whole police station full of weapons and the keys to go with em' but if you don't believe me," Imani looked at Jada and nodded.

Jada raced toward the window holding a silver canister in her hand. Keeping her fingers wrapped around the handle before she pulled the pin and tossed it through the open window. The can banged and dinged along the ground rolling between sneakers and shoes before the gray smog took over the front of the building.

"What the hell is..." One man covered his face as he started to cough, "That!"

"Tear gas, bitch!" Jada shouted before closing

the window back, "That'll buy us about 30 minutes, I doubt anyone brought any milk with them."

The mob, once looking for blood, quickly started looking for an escape as they scattered. The common goal fell to the wayside for their own personal safety.

"You whores won't get away with this!" Susan screamed. She tugged at her zip ties but there was no release from the hogtie that the duo put her in. Letting her sit in Precious' dry blood.

Imani rolled her eyes and sucked her teeth, "I was hoping you were dead."

"My son's gonna come for me and when he does, he's gonna make you bleed," Susan hissed. Imani looked over at Jada for a moment and then looked back at Susan before sending a fist right into the old woman's mouth, knocking her head back into the tile floor.

"She's not wrong..." Imani looked back up at Jada whose focus was on the crowd of people running from the gas. She could see Richardson and Bowman standing by the crashed truck, looking on at the madness that was unfolding, "They're gonna come in here." Imani stood up and nodded before walking toward the door, Jada turned her head back toward Imani, "Where are you going?"

"I'm gonna make sure we're ready when they do," Imani said.

Jada hurried over to Imani and grabbed her hand, the two stood there for a moment before Jada softly said, "I wish we did it sooner, before all this."

Imani smiled and kissed Jada's fingers, "Look at big bad Jada, all sprung."

Jada pulled her hand back and laughed, "Girl

bye! I'm gonna make sure maniac cop's mommy doesn't go anywhere." Jada leaned over and grabbed a M4 that was leaning by the door and handed it to Imani, "You do what you got to do."

"What 'We' got to do, ain't gonna be pretty," Imani said.

Jada looked back at the blood stained floor that Susan was passed out on, "They don't deserve pretty."

Imani took off down the small hallway toward the janitor's closet, she pulled open the door and stared at the wall of cleaning products before the lights to the building went out, leaving the women in complete darkness. Imani reached into her pocket and pulled out her cellphone to light up the closet once again. The radio came up to Imani's lips and she sighed as she pressed the button, "You cutting the power might be considered some shit I don't like," Imani said.

"That's tough, let me tell you how this is gonna go down," Richardson said, he cracked his neck like he was being filmed for an action movie before pushing down the button, "I'm gonna come in there and I'll put a hole in you and that other little rug gobbler and then I'm gonna piss on your bodies."

"Oooh, someone's kinky. What else do you like, Officer Richardson?" Imani asked.

"I liked cutting your little girlfriend's head off or were you dating the other one? Is this some kind of sister wife thing?" Richardson asked.

"Fuck you," Imani hissed.

"Now who's being kinky?" Richardson asked.

Officer Bowman held down the button on his

radio and smiled, "Listen, how about this? Since I know you've been through a lot tonight. All you have to do is give us Susan and that cell phone and we'll call it square." Richardson started to protest but Bowman put his finger to his lip and winked, "How does that sound to you, sweetheart."

Imani nodded as she started to drop the cleaning products into the mop bucket, "Sounds like you're full of shit," she said to herself. Imani pushed the button down on the radio, "We're gonna need a car."

"I can make that happen," Officer Bowman said.

"You promise if we let you in and hand over Honey BooBoo, you'll let us leave?" Imani asked.

"Susan and the cell phone and you're free," Officer Bowman said.

Imani wheeled the bucket back to the room with Jada and she pressed the button on the radio, "Pull the car up and come get your old lady."

The radio fell silent and Richardson slammed his hand on the hood of the car, "What the hell was all that?"

"Relax, it's just to put the little shits at ease. Once we get your Mama and that phone, it's over for them," Officer Bowman said, he looked around the parking lot and sighed, "Now, see if one of these fine people can lend us their car, since they wanted to get involved so badly."

Laura wasn't too happy about lending her car out to Richardson, but he told her he would do that thing she likes, the next time they go out and no one ever does that thing she likes, not ever, so it seemed like a good trade. The small station wagon pulled up to the front of the police station and parked in the blood at the base of the steps. Everyone's feet had been in and out of all that blood the whole night, leaving red footprints all throughout the parking lot, the whole town was covered in it. Richardson got out of the car, leaving it idling while he pumped his shotgun and stared at Officer Bowman.

"This plan better work, boss," Richardson said.

"Richardson, I would never let anything happen to your Mama. We'll go in, secure her, that phone and then..." Bowman pumped his shotgun, "Put an end to this."

An 'end' is a funny thing. Everyone wants an ending to something, an end to the work day, an end to suffering, an end to this night. That's what was wanted by both sides, but each of them knew as Richardson and Bowman unlocked the front doors to the station and walked in, that the only end was a cold and bloody one. The door pushed open into the darkness of the station. Richardson turned on his flashlight as he slowly led the way into the building.

With each slow step there was a light splash and a strong aroma that pushed up from the floor, "What the hell is that smell?" Officer Bowman asked.

Richardson's black boots slipped out from under him. The flashlight went sailing into the air. As Richardson's back slammed into the floor, his finger pulled back on the trigger and a loud blast filled the room.

"Fuck!" Richardson shouted as he rolled over in the darkness. On all fours he crawled toward the flash light. Richardson stanched the light from the floor and pushed himself to his feet. His fingers came up to his nose and he sniffed. Water started to rush from his eyes as a strong scent of bleach burned his nostrils, "You stupid bitches!" The light pointed toward the open doorway to the hall, "I'm gonna slit them like pigs, you hear that! I'm gonna slit you like fucking pigs!" Richardson moved forward, splashing through the bleach soaked floor, until he heard it. His anger had blocked it from his attention but now it was too loud to ignore. A deep, wet, sucking sound. The beam of the flashlight slowly started to scan the room. The sound grew louder and more frantic as the light came onto a set of black boots. Richardson rushed over only to shine a clear light on his darkest moment. Officer Bowman's body lay there in a pool of blood. The light shone on the massive wound that was the left side of Bowman's face. What was left of his jaw trembled up and down as his tongue slapped against the bloody flesh. Blood pooled in the back of Bowman's throat. And as Bowman attempted to pull in air, he pulled in blood and flesh and released a chilling sound like a broken pipe. Richardson shook his head as he started to back up from Bowman's body, "Fuck! Fuck! Fuck!"

The radios on Bowman and Richardson's hip crackled, "You alright, Mama's boy? I thought I heard you scream." Richardson took hold of the radio and tossed it across the room. The hard black plastic exploded upon connecting with the wall. Richardson placed the shotgun up and continued toward the doorway, slowly placing one foot in front of the other until he was at the doorway. Richardson's boots splashed through the wet tiles as he made his way to the interrogation room. With his back on the wall, Richardson took in some of the stale chemical filled air into his lungs.

The officer quickly spun into the room with the barrel pointed to kill. Hoping for two targets, two manifestations of everything that was wrong with the world, that he could blow away. But instead the light shined on a body, with its head buried into a yellow mop bucket. The big heap of flesh and bone just slumped there. Wrist handcuffed. Legs bound. Richardson creeped into the room, sending ripples through the liquid that lined the floor. The closer he got the heavier the fumes became. Richardson held the shotgun in his right hand and placed his left hand on the blue collar of the body. He knew who it was before he raised her head out the bucket, but he did it anyway.

"Mama?" Richardson said softly.

Susan's red and blistered skin broke free of the bucket of bleach and other industrial cleaning products. Susan's head hung back, letting her jaw run slack. Nothing but ripped and bloody flesh sat behind open teeth, the liquid had eaten away her tongue and lips.

"Sorry she can't tuck you in, but maybe you'll see her in hell!" Imani tossed a match into the room and Richardson watched the flame dance with the foams. Then bucket and his mother were taken over by flames. Richardson's hand raised his shotgun but before he could pull the trigger, the flames overtook him as well. Imani slammed the metal door shut.

"Hurry up!" Jada shouted. The duo raced through the lobby. The doors pushed open with so much force the glass shattered as the doorframe bounced into the brick wall of the building. Imani slid over the hood of the car that sat at the base of the stairs. Jada quickly jumped into the passenger seat, "Drive!"

Imani put the car into drive and pressed her foot to the gas only to come to a quick stopped when Bowman's body crashed down onto the windshield of car.

"Yooou...stuuuu....bittt" Bowman's half a jaw hung freely, snapping and dropping as Office Bowman did his best to release the anger and pain that was in his body. Imani stared at the torn flesh of Bowman's face for a moment before Jada lifted her M4 and pointed it.

"ACAB, bitch!" Jada pulled the trigger and a blast filled the car. Bowman's body flew back as the bullet entered his skull and ripped the life free of his body. The corpse dropped onto the parking lot ground and Imani slammed her foot on the gas pedal. The car jolted forward and the first tire rushed over Bowman's chest, the weight of the vehicle pressed down, cracking ribs which in turn ripped through lung tissue. The body twisted and crumbled under the weight of the car. Bowman's flesh banged against the undercarriage of the car. The body sat still and useless. The back tire slammed into what was left of Bowman's face before crushing his skull and ripping free the last of his flesh.

The car sped off through the parking lot and then cut a sharp U turn, all the while it smeared Bowman's blood and flesh onto the parking lot ground. The headlights of the car blasted into the eyes of the town people. Jada and Imani watched them cover their eyes from the light. Some of them were still red eyed and coughing from the effects of the tear gas. Imani's fingers tightened around the wheel. Jada's hand reached over and took Imani's right hand into her left. They stared at each other for a moment and then Imani's foot pushed down on the gas. The car went roaring forward. A few people were wise enough to jump out of the path of the oncoming car, but others were either too dumb or too stubborn to allow Imani and Jada their freedom.

Metal connected with flesh and bone. A body tumbled into what was left of the windshield sending the netted glass forward toward Imani & Jada's faces but they didn't stop. They didn't slow down. Not when the screaming started. Not as limbs and bodies ripped free from the hellish jaws that the car and the asphalt created. No they never stopped, they just kept driving down that old town road and into the darkness of the night.

Hours passed and the moon gave way to the sun, causing Jada to wake up. The windshield had been kicked out hours ago, so the fresh morning air was hitting them both in the face. Blood stained the inside and outside of the car. Jada looked at Imani who's eyes were glued to the road, trying to forget the madness behind them.

A red and blue glow took over Imani's face and then the sirens started, "Don't stop," Jada said.

Imani looked behind her to see an officer on a motorcycle, "We're gonna have to stop at some point," Imani said. She slowly started to guide the car off to the side of the road and sat there with her hands on the wheel.

The strong footsteps of the officer echoed in the back of Imani's mind. Jada wanted to run, to escape now before she could never escape again, but all they did was sit there staring out the busted windshield. The officer looked at the car and then tapped on Imani's window. Imani turned and started to roll down the window with its handle.

"Are you two alright? What the hell happ-" the words and all thought came to a stop as a pickup truck side swapped Imani and Jada. The officer felt pain for a quick moment before the impact ripped his upper body and lower body apart. The officer's torso tumbled into Imani's lap as the car was forced off the road and into the high grasses along the side.

Imani stared at the bloody torso of the officer. Her legs felt warm and slick as the blood covered her. She pushed at his belt, the only thing keeping his intestines in place, but as Imani pushed the torso, the intestines quickly unraveled onto the floor.

Jada's head bashed into the passenger window. Blood poured free from her scalp, she went to push her door open only to find it jammed. The base of the door was buried deep in the dirt. Jada looked over at Imani who was focused on the blood pouring from the officer's body, then Jada saw him. The driver door of the truck pushed open and out came scorched clothing and burned flesh, holding a gasoline container.

Richardson moved slowly toward the car, every step sent jolts through his body like he was trying to cross the short distance over broken glass. The morning breeze was like razors as it kissed each section of burned flesh on his skin. Richardson stopped and started to unscrew the top of the container. The cap dropped into the dirt and Richardson ignored the pain of his flesh that had fused with his uniform, ripping as he started to pour the gasoline onto the hood of the car.

Jada started to push the door harder into the dirt, "No, no!"

Imani looked up from the blood to see Richardson making his way toward her side. The container raised up and gasoline began to pour onto Imani. She twisted as the cold liquid hit her skin and as she turned she realized that she was pinned. The driver side of the car had caved in, pinning Imani to her seat.

Richardson tossed the empty container to the side and then pushed his hand into his pocket. Charred skin peeled free from Richardson's hand as he searched for his lighter.

Jada quickly ran her hands down the bloody torso of the dead officer and pulled his service pistol from its holster. When she looked back,

Richardson was standing there with the lighter in his bloody hand.

"See yoooou in....helll-"

Bang

Bang

Bang

Richardson's words were cut short by Jada pumping three rounds into his chest, "Remain silent, motherfucker!" Jada shouted. The gun dropped to the floor and Jada rested her head back.

"Are we still going to the Essence festival?" Imani asked.

Jada looked over at her and then looked forward and closed her eyes, "Shut up."

The End

NEIGHBOR

"Don't forget to take the trash out."

Malcolm sighed at the trash can and then rolled his eyes. "If you remembered, why didn't you do it?" He mumbled.

Rachel's head popped out from around the corner, "What you say?"

Malcolm jumped, "Damn, nothing."

"Yeah, that's what I thought you said." Rachel laughed, "Maybe if you move fast enough I'll reward you with that thing you like."

Malcolm quickly pulled the bag out of the can and tied the loops into a knot, "Say less."

Rachel's laughter filled the kitchen as Malcolm opened the door to the garage. His fingers hit the light switch, the click filled his ears but he was still in darkness.

"The light's out-" Malcolm looked back into the kitchen but Rachel was long gone. Getting ready for another night in their very first home. It had only been a month since they moved in but everything was going amazingly well... aside from the yard, that was a monster that Malcolm had no idea how to tame.

Through the darkness, he could see the glowing button for the garage door. Malcolm pushed it and the grinding and cranking filled up the house as the garage door roared to life, lifting up. Malcolm ducked under the door and stepped into the darkness of the front of the house. He tossed the bag into the trash can and pulled it up the driveway.

"Hello, neighbor." The voice ripped through the silence of the night, and Malcolm stopped cold. He glanced up, and standing at the top of his driveway was a figure.

"Frank?" Malcolm awkwardly laughed, "You scared the piss out of me. Don't be sneaking up on Black folks like that." Malcolm continued to pull the trash up the steep driveway.

The closer he got the more detail Malcolm could make out. Unless Frank had lost fifty pounds and grown a foot, the man at the top of the driveway wasn't Frank.

Malcolm stopped.

"Hello..." the man's left arm came up slowly and he waved, back and forth, but it looked so mechanical. Malcolm peered closer and as he watched the man waving he could see a painfully large grin on the man's face, "Neighbor!" The man's right hand came up with an eight-inch kitchen knife.

"Shit!" Malcolm didn't let the word hit the cool night air before he turned around to run back to the house, but standing right in front of the garage was a woman, her bright white teeth shined in the moonlight as she stood there with a machete in her hand, waving at Malcolm.

"Neighbor!" The word ripped free from her throat in one jagged motion. Malcolm turned and ran into the tall grass of the yard he kept swearing he would get to. The figures were frantically running behind him with their blades shining in the moonlight and their smiles never fading. They were stretched along their faces like some kind of demonically positive mask.

Malcolm ran up to his back door, his hands twisted the knob but the door didn't give way. They might have been the only people in the neighborhood who locked their doors. "Get the fuck away from me," Malcolm shouted as he pulled the grill between him and the two freaks.

"Hello, neighbor!" The male with the massive kitchen knife slashed forward. The grill and man both crumbled to the ground, but Malcolm had no time to celebrate because the woman's machete came down fast to his left. The sound of metal cracking into stone filled the night.

Malcolm turned back around running through the massive yard thinking he could make it to the front door or a side window. "Baby!" Malcolm screamed. He jumped the bush at the end of his yard. His knees slammed into the ground, there was give and somewhat of a softness to the grass but then a ripple of pain rushed through his body. Malcolm's knee had landed right on the metal head of his garden hose.

"Fuck!" Malcolm looked down at his bloody knee, the kneecap was to the side of his leg. He placed his hand on it and another jolt of pain ripped through his body.

"Hello Neighbor." Malcolm looked up to see a

crowd of smiling faces slowly making their way from his front yard to him.

Malcolm crawled backward as much as his leg would allow only to bump into the knees of the woman and the man. Malcolm looked up and their smiling faces came down quickly, pinning Malcolm to the ground.

"Get off of me!" Malcolm shouted.

Malcolm took a swing, connecting with the man's jaw and knocking him to the ground. Before he could even think of doing the same to the woman, she rammed the machete into Malcolm's bicep. The blade cut through his flesh, severing tendons, craving along the bone, leaving its mark until the tip was driven into the dirt. She had spiked Malcom in place with the machete.

There was too much pain running through Malcolm's body and mind for him to fully process what was going on, he felt he was having a fever dream or his first glimpse into hell. The woman straddled Malcolm, her hands ran up his shirt until her nails were digging into his chest.

"What do you want!" Malcolm screamed.

The woman's smile quickly dropped and she stared at Malcolm with a blank look, dead of any and all emotion. The woman tilted her head back and as she did that, Malcolm could see something pushing free of her stomach, it was almost as if there was a baby that was kicking itself free. But then the movement went from her stomach to her chest. Then it made its way to her neck, which swelled to three times its normal size as she tried to pass this massive object through her throat.

"Oh my God!" Malcolm shouted as the

woman's head snapped forward and her jaw expanded to reveal a large black maggot squirming its way out of her body. Slime dripped down onto Malcolm as the maggot got closer to his face. Malcolm turned his head frantically left and right. He kept his lips pressed tight, but then two hands locked onto his head and forced him to be still. Then the woman's finger clawed at Malcolm's lips trying to rip his jaw open. Blood and broken nails. Burning lips and shattered teeth. All of that only kept Malcolm safe for a moment, until those bony fingers got into his mouth and ripped his jaw down. The woman leaned in her mouth pinned open with the massive maggot coming out.

Malcolm's eyes were wide as the maggot first touched his tongue. The slime filled every corner of his mouth. The maggot's body twisted and turned as it forced its way down Malcolm's throat. There was no air. No screams. Just tears and pains.

* * *

The lights in the bedroom went out as did the TV. "What the fuck?" Rachel said as she looked around the room. She had just stepped out of the shower and squeezed into that pink and white teddy lingerie that Malcolm liked. Rachel sat on her knees in the middle of the bed waiting. "Malcolm!" The bedroom door pushed open and Rachel sighed, "What took you so long? The power went out." She bounced a little on her heels, "But maybe we can worry about that later?" Rachel's hands went out and then she laughed. "Why are you smiling like that?" The bedroom door closed... "Malcolm? Malcolm? Malcolm!"

PARISH

Please Review

DON'T TELL GRANDMA

I hate it here. The food is weird; the beds are hard, and the smell of mothballs chokes out any other scent. However, when you're an only child with two parents who had you too soon in their marriage, you don't have a choice of where you spend your summers.

"Grandma! I don't see it!"

Who keeps dog food on the top shelf when they're not even five feet tall? How was she going to get this if I wasn't here? Even I had to stand on the counter. Pasta, rice, beans, rat...

"Rat!"

The pain of my arm crashing through the glass dining table hit me before I even realized I had fallen. Tears flooded my eyes as I looked up at the fury little demon. It was still, so still I thought it was, and then like an evil Jack-in-the-box, it sprung to life and started racing through the cabinets, knocking over cans. I didn't stay to see what else it could do; I ran in a panic.

"Daniel!" A shriek came from the back room.

My eyes stayed locked on the kitchen entrance

as I backed up the narrow hallway. The mothball scent pushed free of every open door I passed. Old pictures of a time and people who were long departed lined the walls as I recoiled deeper into the hall.

"Grandma," I whispered.

My hand went behind me and it searched for the cool door knob. When the metal brushed against my fingers, I saw the dirty rat break free from the kitchen and run wildly into the living room. I pushed open the door and bolted into the room, slamming the door behind me. My head rested on the wood and I closed my eyes as I attempted to get a hold of myself to explain to the old relic that her house was under attack by a demon rat. She'll swear I let it in or I was seeing things.

"Grandma... there's a-"

Something ripped the words from my lips as I felt a bag of weight leap onto my back and latch on like a cowboy riding a bull. Leather, thin skin pressed against my cheek as I spun and twisted to break free. I could see my grandma sitting in her bed, staring in shock and horror. Behind her, in her big bedroom mirror, was me with a 96-pound naked old woman latched onto my back. She smelled of Icy Hot, mothballs, and blood.

"Daniel!" Grandma shouted.

The woman's bony fingers pressed into my shoulders like nails into a coffin, and her head swung back. I watched it all in the mirror. Her blood-stained jaws parted to reveal perfectly shaped bloody teeth.

"She's got them veneers!" Grandma shouted.

She twisted to get out of bed, the first attempt I've ever seen. "Leave my grandson alone, Betty!"

Betty's bloody veneers came down and locked onto my ear. I screamed when I felt the bright white pain rush through my body. Betty pulled her head back and took my ear with her. I dropped to my knees out of the mirror's view as Betty nibbled up my ear like a strip of bacon. I could smell Betty's bloody peppermint scent, mouth coming close again, but this time grandma stopped her, swinging a metal pan into her face. Betty went flying back along with a stream of cold yellow liquid.

"She bit me! She bit me!" I shouted.

"What the hell is wrong with you, Betty? You know we can't bite our guest. Frank just got kicked out for that," Grandma said.

While I'm sure the story of Frank and his banishment from the nursing home was riveting, I had too many other things on my mind. Like one, I was missing an ear, which meant my life was over. Two, I was covered in my grandma's smelly, cold piss, which meant my life was over. And three, which was the most important, Betty was on her feet and staring at me like a hungry dog staring at a steak which meant my life was over. Pack it up, we're done.

"We need to go, Grandma," I said.

"No! Betty needs to go," she said and swung her bedpan from side to side, fanning the thick scent of urine deeper into my nostrils.

I wanted to gag, but Betty took a step forward, so I ripped the bedpan free of Grandma's hands and slammed it square into Betty's nose. Blood splashed forward as her paper-thin skin exploded on impact. Betty dropped to the floor, and I mounted her. She was the bull now. I started whaling down onto her with the bloody and dented bedpan. Smacks and cracks filled my eardrums until I felt my grandma's hands on my blood-covered knuckles.

"That's enough, Daniel... she's dead," Grandma said.

I sat still on Betty's chest and stared down at what used to be her face; it reminded me of my mom's cherry cobbler, but instead of the sweet smell of cherries and cinnamon; it was blood and piss.

"I hate it here, Grandma," I finally said it out loud for the world to hear.

Grandma patted me on the shoulder and nodded. "I hate it here too, sweetie. This is the fourth time this happened today... Paula said the mailman tried to eat her today. Can you believe it? The mailman! I need to lock these damn windows and have you fed Biscuit yet?"

The dog! I quickly pulled open the door and raced to the living room, only to see Biscuit staring at that dirty rat. Biscuit ripped it in two, but it still crawled toward me, pulling rancid-smelling blood behind it. The other half was nowhere in sight. I stared at Biscuit, who tilted his head at my missing ear. Then he burped up black fur.

"Don't tell Grandma," I whispered.

DEAD SOIL PREVIEW

I sprung to life in total darkness as I clawed at my neck. A hard collar had my body fighting to breathe. My tongue sat heavy, weighted down by a metallic sting as I pulled myself away from choking on my blood. I sprung forward, ripping the chains as far as they could go. I forced my jaw open past the pain to release the blood, letting it pool between my chained feet.

"You slept through most of it." A soft voice beside me caused my eyes to fully open and adjust to the darkness that surrounded me. It woke me up to the darkness and the cries. Chains banging and people calling out for their Gods, "I feared the fever had gotten you."

My eyes settled on the blur in the darkness. "My grandfather." I let the words creep free from my burning throat.

"Dead or chained... both are the same."

I listened to the cries of broken voices hidden within the darkness.

"Let us go."

"Mama! Mama!"

"Death! Death upon you, upon your children, and your children's children!"

"It burns, it burns." That whisper pulled my attention away from one blur and into the foul smell of another. "It burns." A weak man's voice called out. Vomit and shit clouded my senses as weak hands came toward me. "It burns." I allowed his bloody fingers to wrap around mine and I clasped them.

"It's going to be all right," I whispered.

"No, no, it's not," the soft voice that greeted me from the darkness replied. I knew that voice, I've heard it before... it was a woman, but who I couldn't place. She had given up hope or come to terms with what our fate would be, but that didn't mean we all had to.

The roar of the ocean was a foreign to me. I listened to it crash against the wood, drowning out the screams of those around me. I closed my eyes and held the pair of boney fingers tightly in my own as I rested my head back, releasing the pinch of the chains against my skin. My mother once told me Mother Nature sings to you in many ways, from the birds in the morning to the sounds of the night and this, the sea fighting the sounds in my head.

"Where are they taking us?" I whispered into the darkness.

"No place good. No place warm or beautiful like home," the soft voice whispered back. I heard her crying, low, sad sounds coming from lips like my own, scared and bloody. "He's dead, you know that?"

My hands shook the frail frame of the bloody fingered man, against the wood and the more I shook the more warmth covered me, the slick warmth of blood covered everything until his body slipped free of my hold and he crumbled against the wood in a heap.

"We'll be joining him soon. Free from this and carried away in death's arms," the soft voice whispered.

"Free?" A loud creek flooded the dark before a glow appeared, revealing one of the pale men slowly walking down the steps. A light shined on him from up above, and he held a light in his hand and a metal pitcher in the other. The light was a fire hugged and carried by glass and metal. My fingers slipped back into the warmth of the frail man's body. "Free... we will be free," I whispered to myself.

The pale man shouted things into the darkness and the many voices answered with the same cries and curses as before. We didn't understand his tongue. Yet, they hoped he could understand theirs. Feel the pain in our voices and set us free if asked. I stared at the light that carried his twisted face through the darkness and I knew there was no hope or safety to be found in that man. No point wasting my voice to ask for anything. My fingers pushed along the slickness. I used my nails to rip and scrap away at the flesh. The warmth tickled my fingertips.

"What is he doing?" The soft voice asked.

The pale man had pulled a chained man from the darkness and into the light that shined from his caged flame. The man fought the best he could, but the chains made him weaker, kept him slower. They kept him still, much like me. The shouts of pain were no longer hidden in the dark. The pale man's fist beat into the man's face. Once and then again, and again. Each time his fist would come back into the light of the flame, it brought with it blood and then it shot back into the darkness for more blood, like a vampire bat. The pale man rested his caged flame down to the floor, allow us all to see the torn flesh and swollen eyes of his victim.

"What is he doing?" That woman's sweet voice ripped free of the darkness to ask again. My fingers continued to scrape and rip. Flesh gave way to my nails as I dragged them down and along the bone. The caged flame, the only light in the darkness, seemed to have grabbed all our attention. The pale man stood tall behind the broken man. He pulled at the leather wrapped around his waist and let his clothes fall to his feet, baring himself to us and the darkness.

"What is he doing?" The screaming started and chains rattled, and I turned my head away from the sight and focused on the bone that slipped through my bloody fingers. I dug my nails deeper into the flesh, just as the pale man buried himself deeper. My fingers wrapped around the bone and through the screams and cries of my people, I pulled and pulled until the bone snapped free.

The pale man shouted and laughed, his gold tooth shining in the light, as his flesh pounded on the flesh of the broken, pushing himself deeper inside of the man. I held the bone in my hand and worked on the chains that wrapped around my body.

"Leave him!"
"Let him go!"
"Monster!"

Screams ripped free of the darkness and surrounded the light of the caged flame. The pale man was smiling, lost in the pleasure he was receiving from forcing himself into a shattered man. He pulled himself free of the man's flesh and spat on him, slowly reaching down to get dressed. The whole time, he smiled. As he did his deed, he smiled. As he wiped his sweat and seed on the broken man, he smiled. Even as I drove that jagged bone into his neck, he smiled... if only for a moment. I buried the stained white bone deep into his unwilling body, and he fought and twisted. His limbs tried to break free from the hold I had on him. Blood gushed from his body and bathed my skin. As he grew limp in my arms, I knew there would be far more blood before the night was over.

. . .

"You killed him, you killed him!" Shouts from the darkness surrounded me. The rattle of chains followed as hands rested on me. I wondered if they could feel the blood of freedom on me.

"It's the witch doctor's boy... Dayo's mate."

"You've used your magic to set us free?" The darkness asked.

I trudged up to the caged flame and held the jagged bloody bone to the light. "No magic, but we will be free. Bring your chains to me." I looked over at the pale man, whose blood was filling up the floor and soaking into the wood. "And someone bring me..." I shot my bloody finger at the pale man's body, "his bones!"

The wood moaned as the chains dropped from one body after another. The crashing of the sea against the boat drowned everything else out. If there was ever a sign that Mother Nature approved of what we were about to do, of the blood her children were about to seek, it was the amount of effort she put into concealing our escape. Masking our steps with thunder and waves as we traveled up the steps to the unknown. I could hear them laughing and tossing out sounds in a tongue none of us understood. The only thing I hoped to hear from their pale lips were the screams we would rip from them.

"What now?" That soft voice came up behind me. I looked over my shoulder at her brown eyes and the sea of brown eyes behind her. They called her Dayo, the beauty from my tribe, who had been promised to me. So we could build the family, Grandfather begged for. My people held their chains tightly in their hands, as my fingers wrapped around the stained white rib bones of two different men. One wicked, one broken, both helping me in my time of need.

I turned my head toward the wooden doors and placed my fist on them. "We fight until they die, or we die, or both," I whispered. I pushed the doors open, letting their laughter surround us as our feet slapped onto the cool wooden floor of the boat. Wet spots along the wood eased the pains in my feet as I slowly crept toward the laughter. A sea of brown eyes followed behind me, until I pushed another door open to reveal the pale men all seated among one another, drinking and eating. Enjoying life as if they didn't have bodies hidden in the belly of this watery devil!

As we stood in the doorway, the laughter died, replaced by shouts and screams. Then a sword ripped free and swung through the air and, just like that, I was in a fight for my life, for my freedom, and for my people's freedom.

"Them! Us! Or both!" Dayo shouted, as she and the rest of our army rushed in with their chains swinging. I saw a metal rod raised toward us, much like it did toward my grandfather. I leaped forward, bones sharp and ready. Before the blast could rip me free of this world and send me into another, I drove the tips of my bones into the eyes of the pale man. They were small white plums that popped open easily, taking in all the bone and spurting blood into the air. The pale man screamed in my new favorite language of pain, and I dragged the bones out, ripping free what was left of his eyes from his head.

My bloody hands went to the pale man's sword and then I rushed into battle with my people. "Kill them all!" I swung my sword forward, the blade connecting with another pale man's blade.

"No surrender!" Dayo screamed. Her chains were wrapped around the neck of a bearded, pale man. Her body latched to him like an anaconda to its prey. She tightened the chain and his neck turned from the pale white to a dark red and then dark purple. I watched his hands flailing around, but then my mind was pulled back to my own fight as I received a boot to the chest. The wooden floor roughly kissed every bit of my skin. The sword danced along the wood until it stopped at a pair of bare, bloody feet.

My eyes traveled up the blood-stained feet, following a trail of red along twitching flesh. The man couldn't keep still. His legs shook like trees during a great wind. As my eyes watched his arms and neck snap from one unnatural angle to another, I saw it:

The hole that I had created in his chest as I dug for my freedom. His white eyes settled upon me. He threw his body forward with no care for his life. His jaw snapped back and forth. I forced my hands into his neck to keep his teeth at bay.

"The devil!"

"It cannot be." the fighting stopped. Everyone who was battling for their lives turned to focus on the doorway. Everyone but me because my fight had just begun. I squeezed, pressing my fingers into his brown flesh. He kept pushing forward, his hands dragging along my skin. His nails ripped flesh free from my body like I once did his. His jaws snapped like the jaws of a hungry lion. Then a blast filled the room and blood rained from the dead man's head as he tumbled off me. I pushed free of the body. Crawling away from the scene as quickly as I could. I searched for the helping hand that saved me, only to see a young pale boy holding a smaller smoking metal rod in his hand. I choked on the smoke and scent of shit that filled the room. The boy stared at me, then he looked back at the doorway, and I saw just what everyone else saw. The pale devil, who came with his caged flame, stood in the doorway. His head bent so far that his ear rested permanently on his shoulder. Blood still poured from the jagged hole in his neck, dark red dripping onto the wood and pooling at his feet.

"The devil," I whispered, and then the dead man who was once upon me twitched and jerked. His legs kicked in the air until his broken body was back on its feet. He stared at me with those lifeless eyes that he shared with death and tilted his head to the side. Blood drained free of the hole in the man's skull and then a metal ball fell free from the large hole in the side of his head. It bounced along the wooden floor and then the pale devil and the dead man shot forward, teeth tearing into any flesh that they could find. I leaned over a table and grabbed another sword, because the fight for my life had become far, far deadlier than I could imagined.

Dead Soil Coming This September From DarkLit Press

AFTERWORD

Thank you for picking this up and checking out my attempt at extreme horror. I had fun with this, as you can see, I still can't leave the jokes out, but that's just me.

This really means a lot to me, because this story is the first one I'm wrote and sold exclusively on my site (That's no longer the case). So to know that you picked this without me having the backing of some billion dollar company behind me, really means the world.

If you have any thoughts about this story or want to pick up more of my work feel free to message me on social media, email me or check out my shop.

https://bio.site/Sylvesterbarzey

About the Author

Hey Survivor!

My name is Sylvester Barzey and I am a best selling horror and fantasy author. I grew up in Bronx, NY, lived in the smallest state in the country for a while and then transplanted to Lawrence, GA.

I'm a military veteran with an addiction to all things horror. My overall goal is to shine a spotlight on BIPOC characters within the horror/fantasy genre. From a young age I was obsessed with horror movies, mostly slashers. The mythos of the "Final Girl" trope was always something that appealed to me. The act of taking someone and watching them overcome the greatest odds to be the ultimate survivor has been a strong attraction to the horror for me.

But, what I didn't realize growing up was all these survivors were White. Seeing only one type of person rise, builds blocks within people's minds, it causes them to think that surviving is a trait only in one race, which is far from the truth. The Black community (Black Women for sure) have survival built into their DNA. History has shown us that overcoming great odds is something Black people have always done.

Being that I couldn't find the final girls I was looking for (There are some don't get me wrong and they are amazing), I set out to create them. I want to produce Black heroes who overcome world shattering events and rise above them. My goal is for people to say Catherine Briggs' name in the same breath as they say Sidney Prescott and Laurie Strode. It's my mission to change horror so that my children can look at it and see themselves as survivors.

Random Facts:

I love The Golden Girls

I wonder what people taste like

I hate the snow

My Top Five Movies Are:

Scream, Candyman, Day of The Dead, Train To Busan & Mulan

Reach out to me by Author@sylvester-barzey.com or visit his www.sylvesterbarzey.com

- facebook.com/authorsylvesterbarzey
- x.com/sylvesterbarzey
- instagram.com/sylvesterbarzey
- goodreads.com/sbgoodreads
- bookbub.com/authors/sbarzeybookbub
- amazon.com/author/sylvesterbarzey

Also by Sylvester Barzey

If you enjoyed this book please be sure to review it and tell a friend.

Don't worry the ride isn't over:

Planet Dead

Planet Dead 2: Patient Zero

Planet Dead 3

The Realm

Stitches

Young Blood

Get Your Free Planet Dead Novel: Love Bites Today

More Books At:

www.sylvesterbarzey.com/books

If that isn't enough zombie and horror madness for you, then become a "Survivor Among The Living" an all exclusive newsletter and secret website for zombie & horror lovers. Win prizes, read sneak peeks, and survivor the outbreak with Catherine and other like minded crazy people.

Join Today

Also join "Sylvester Barzey's Fan Club" for prizes, updates and a look inside the author's mind.

Join Today

Learn More At www.sylvesterbarzey.com

Printed in Great Britain
by Amazon